PRAISE FOR

EINSTEIN
THE CLASS HAMSTER

"This hamster is almost as smart as I am."
—ALBERT EINSTEIN

"These illustrations are amazing! And done by a
teenager! I'm buying this book for all my friends!"
—JOHN SULLIVAN, JAKE'S COUSIN

"The story is so funny, I did several spit-takes."
—DR. ERIC BROWN, JANET'S DENTIST

"Jake sure buys a lot of pencils."
—TOM LYNCH, OFFICE SUPPLY STORE

Janet Tashjian

TEIN

THE CLASS HAMSTER

Illustrated by
Jake Tashjian

SQUARE
FISH

Christy Ottaviano Books
HENRY HOLT AND COMPANY ~ NEW YORK

TO JOHN OVER–
BEST. TEACHER. EVER.

SQUARE
FISH

An Imprint of Macmillan
175 Fifth Avenue
New York, NY 10010
mackids.com

Our books may be purchased in bulk for promotional, educational, or
business use. Please contact your local bookseller or the Macmillan
Corporate and Premium Sales Department at (800) 221-7945
ext. 5442 or by e-mail at MacmillanSpecialMarkets@macmillan.com.

Library of Congress Cataloging-in-Publication Data
Tashjian, Janet.
Einstein the class hamster / Janet Tashjian ; illustrated by Jake Tashjian.
pages   cm
Summary: Einstein, a very knowledgeable hamster, is desperate to
help the students in his classroom win an audition for a televised trivia
game show but, unfortunately, only one student, Ned, can hear him.
ISBN 978-1-250-07966-4 (paperback)
[1. Questions and answers—Fiction. 2. Hamsters—Fiction. 3. Schools—Fiction.
4. Children's art.] I. Tashjian, Jake, illustrator. II. Title.
PZ7.T211135Ein 2013   [Fic]—dc23   2013018839

Originally published in the United States by Christy Ottaviano Books/
Henry Holt and Company, LLC
First Square Fish Edition: 2016
Book designed by April Ward
Square Fish logo designed by Filomena Tuosto

1 3 5 7 9 10 8 6 4 2

AR: 1.0 / LEXILE: 750L

"I do not like to state an opinion on a matter unless I know the precise facts."

—ALBERT EINSTEIN

"Here's a fact:
Someone needs to clean out my cage!"

—EINSTEIN THE CLASS HAMSTER

CHAPTER ONE

ANSWER THAT QUESTION!

Hello, out there in television land! Welcome to the number one show at Boerring Elementary:

ANSWER THAT QUESTION!

I'm your host, Einstein the class hamster, and today we've got some great contestants:

Ricky

Ned

Bonnie

Our contestants will be competing for some amazing prizes. Tell them what they can win, Marlon.

Sorry about that, folks. Marlon's a turtle, so he's a bit slow.

"Hey!"

Here's what our contestants are competing for today—a shiny new pencil, a box of mints, and a **SHETLAND PONY**! But first, the rules of the game.

I'll be asking several questions, and it's up to our contestants and you in the studio audience to find the correct answer before our time is up. Let's start with a warm-up question. Ready?

Here we GO!

What is the **DEADLIEST ANIMAL** on the planet? Our contestants have ten seconds to answer. Start thinking!

Come on, kids. Let's get those brains working!

Still nothing? Okay, here's a hint:
This animal is deadlier than a shark,

a snake,

or even a lion.

Time's up, folks! The answer is **the MOSQUITO!**

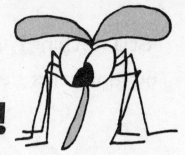

The mosquito may be small but it can be deadly, in some areas spreading malaria, which kills a million people a year. That is one nasty insect!

We'll be right back with more questions after this word from our sponsor. Stay tuned for lots of fun and games on **ANSWER...THAT... QUESTION**.

BRRRRINNNNGGG!

"NO . . . NOT AGAIN!" Einstein shouted.

Okay, students, take out your math books.

"Somebody stop her!" Einstein said. "That woman is ruining my show!"

9

"We'll start with the five table,"
Ms. Moreno continued. "All together—
**5, 10, 15, 20, 25, 30, 35, 40,
45, 50, 55, 60, 65, 70** . . .

THIS IS MY AUDIENCE, NOT YOURS! WHY ARE YOU DOING THIS?

"75, 80, 85, 90, 95, 100."

"Bring out the hook! Get her out of here!" Einstein yelled.

But Ms. Moreno couldn't hear him.

Einstein put down his microphone and settled into his cage.

"Take five, Marlon. On second thought, take six. I now **HATE** the number five."

Ned made sure none of his classmates were watching before he spoke to the hamster. "Einstein, you realize you're the class pet and Ms. Moreno is the teacher, right? That SHE'S the one in charge and you don't really have a game show?

That you keep yelling **ANSWER**...
THAT...**QUESTION** but no one
ever does? That I'm the only kid who
can actually HEAR you?"

"Details, details." Einstein couldn't
believe his show had been interrupted
by THAT WOMAN yet again. "Can I at
least do the Tasty Tidbits segment?"
Einstein asked.

Ned couldn't help but smile. Nothing made Einstein happier than learning new, interesting facts, and Einstein's Tasty Tidbits was the part of the show where he shared those fun facts with his audience to help them prepare for **ANSWER...THAT... QUESTION**.

Einstein loved stumbling on a fun fact more than he loved carrots or kibbles or sunflower seeds, which is why he named the segment Tasty Tidbits. Ned wasn't too sure about the whole dressing up like the fancy women who worked on REAL TV game shows, but it was Einstein's show, not his.

"OF COURSE you can do a Tasty Tidbit," Ned said. "Why do you think I came over here?"

Einstein looked at Ms. Moreno in the front of the class. *She's a no-good ham,* Einstein thought. *Always hogging the spotlight.* But he was a professional, and it was time to end the show.

"You ready?" Ned asked.

When it came to Tasty Tidbits, Einstein was born ready.

EINSTEIN'S TASTY TIDBITS

Believe it or not, the highest concentration of mosquitoes on the planet is NOT in the tropics but in the Arctic tundra. Because it's so flat, when the snow and ice melt, the water has nowhere to go and forms shallow pools that provide breeding grounds for mosquitoes. When you add in the constant sunlight of summer as well as rising temperatures, the pools of warm water make perfect mosquito incubators. BILLIONS can swarm in a day, filling the skies—in the Arctic!

But don't blame the males. Only female mosquitoes bite because they need protein from blood for their eggs. (Regular mosquito diet consists of plant sugar.) It's not the mosquito's bite that makes you itch. It's the body's immune response to the saliva she leaves behind.

CHAPTER TWO

A LITTLE BACKGROUND on EINSTEIN

Einstein comes from a **long line** of class hamsters.

His father, Aristotle, was a class hamster.

Knowledge is power—at least according to Sir Francis Bacon.

His grandmother Banjo was a class hamster.

Even his great-great-great-grandfather Fuzzy was a class hamster.

Because his family spent so much time in classrooms, Einstein learned a lot of facts most hamsters don't know. He knows the capitals of all fifty states:

Montgomery, Alabama

Juneau, Alaska

Phoenix, Arizona

Little Rock, Arkansas

Sacramento, California

Denver, Colorado

Hartford, Connecticut

Dover, Delaware

Tallahassee, Florida

Atlanta, Georgia

Honolulu, Hawaii

Boise, Idaho

Springfield, Illinois

Indianapolis, Indiana

Des Moines, Iowa

Topeka, Kansas

Frankfort, Kentucky

Baton Rouge, Louisiana

Augusta, Maine

Annapolis, Maryland

Boston, Massachusetts

Lansing, Michigan

St. Paul, Minnesota

Jackson, Mississippi

Jefferson City, Missouri

Helena, Montana

Lincoln, Nebraska

Carson City, Nevada

Concord, New Hampshire

Trenton, New Jersey

Santa Fe, New Mexico

Albany, New York

Raleigh, North Carolina

Bismarck, North Dakota

Columbus, Ohio

Oklahoma City, Oklahoma

Salem, Oregon

Harrisburg, Pennsylvania

Providence, Rhode Island

Columbia, South Carolina

Pierre, South Dakota

Nashville, Tennessee

Austin, Texas

Salt Lake City, Utah

Montpelier, Vermont

Richmond, Virginia

Olympia, Washington

Charleston, West Virginia

Madison, Wisconsin

Cheyenne, Wyoming

He loves to learn about history and music.

He loves to make graphs and charts with his ~~poop~~ food.

He loves helping kids learn about math and science and geography.

WHICH IS WHY HE CREATED HIS GAME SHOW IN THE FIRST PLACE.

Einstein based **ANSWER...THAT... QUESTION** on all the study questions his relatives had handed down through the years. **ANSWER...THAT... QUESTION** and Tasty Tidbits were the perfect study guides. He was the school's most valuable resource. SO WHY WEREN'T THEY USING HIM?

With all these interesting facts at his hamster fingertips, Einstein didn't understand why Principal Decker insisted on hiring HUMANS to teach at Boerring Elementary when Einstein could do a better job at a fraction of the salary. (Fractions are also something Einstein knows a lot about.)

Maybe THIS is the year Einstein gets to make his beloved ancestors proud.

EINSTEIN'S TASTY TIDBITS

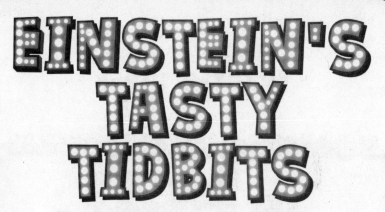

The capital of Texas—AUSTIN—rhymes with the capital of Massachusetts—BOSTON.

CHAPTER THREE

SOME BACKGROUND ON NED

Ned had no idea why he was the only one in Ms. Moreno's class who could hear Einstein. Maybe it was because he had twelve animals of his own that were taking over his house—

2 goldfish

1 golden retriever

3 chickens

1 ferret

3 cats

2 parakeets

Or maybe it was because when he was a baby, Ned had tubes put in his ears that affected his hearing in a way doctors couldn't explain.

Or maybe it was because Ned didn't have a lot of friends and Einstein was the only one in class who seemed to care about what Ned thought. Maybe being such a sensitive kid had an upside—like being able to understand hamsters.

Whatever the reason, Ned liked hanging out with Einstein. Watching the hamster organize his notes for **ANSWER...THAT...QUESTION** was usually the highlight of Ned's day.

Now all Ned had to do was make a few human friends.

EINSTEIN'S TASTY TIDBITS

Ferrets are one of the most popular pets in the United States. The word *ferret* comes from the Latin word *furonem*, which means "thief." Ferrets ARE master thieves, able to steal anything they can grab, so they're often trained to hunt rabbits and other small animals. But they're only master burglars when they're awake—ferrets sleep more than twenty hours a day.

CHAPTER FOUR

THE PRINCIPAL

There was only one person Einstein disliked more than Ms. Moreno, and that was Principal Decker.

STOP RUNNING IN THE HALLS NOW!

The main reason Einstein disliked Principal Decker was that he didn't notice most of what went on in his own school.

- He didn't notice the ivy covering the front door that students had to squeeze through on their way to class every morning.

- He didn't notice Mr. Wright, the janitor, playing poker with students during recess.

- He didn't notice Ms. Moreno spontaneously dozing off several times a day in her classroom.

FOOL   CRETIN   KNUCKLE HEAD   MORON

The school could be under alien attack, and the principal wouldn't pay one bit of attention.

Principal Decker only cared about one thing—

ZZZ

Twinkles the python.

WHAT ARE YOU LOOKING AT?

Twinkles was SUPPOSED to stay in the Science Center, but Principal Decker carried his tank around with him all day. Sometimes he even wore Twinkles around his neck like a scarf.

But Einstein had to give Twinkles credit: He didn't just attempt to gobble Einstein up; the snake was creative in the ways he tried to devour him.

"I've got something caught between my teeth," Twinkles would say. "Do you think you could check it out?" As if Einstein were some kind of rodent dental floss.

"My uvula's swollen," Twinkles said another time. "Would you mind giving it a quick look?"

UVULA

Einstein planned to stay as far away from Twinkles as possible.

EINSTEIN'S TASTY TIDBITS

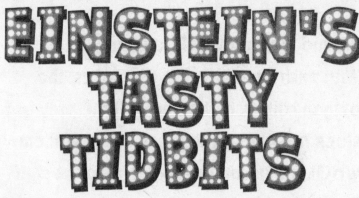

Pythons live in humid areas like Asia and Africa. They average around fifteen feet in length, but some types have grown to be as long as thirty-seven feet. Pythons squeeze the life out of their prey, usually wild animals like antelope, monkeys, caimans, and lizards. They are constrictors who coil themselves around their prey before eating them. With each breath their victim takes, the python coils itself tighter until the prey stops breathing. Then they swallow them WHOLE, digesting everything except stuff like eggshells, beaks, fur, and feathers. Those indigestible items wind up as snake poop. The bigger the meal, the longer it takes to digest, so sometimes a python needs to eat only four or five times a year.

CHAPTER FIVE

A SPECIAL GUEST

Einstein decided his show needed a remote segment with a special guest to boost ratings.

He knew none of the students could hear him, but when he was singing the song he made up about prefixes and suffixes a few nights ago, he could've sworn the custodian was humming along.

Maybe Mr. Wright was just waiting for an invitation to appear on **ANSWER...THAT...QUESTION**.

"Ladies and gentlemen, I'd like to introduce Mr. Wright, the custodian of our wonderful school. Mr. Wright, say hello to the people at home!"

But Mr. Wright didn't say a thing.

"Mr. Wright, since you're in charge of the school's recycling program, you should be an expert on today's segment of **ANSWER...THAT... QUESTION**!"

Silence.

"Here's your first question: If a can ISN'T recycled, it can sit around and clutter up the planet for how long? Take your time, Mr. Wright."

More silence.

"Any guesses? One year? Two? The

answer is 100 years! That's a long time, don't you agree?"

Mr. Wright continued to mop up the vomit in the hallway.

"Maybe you'll have better luck with this next question. Ready? If an aluminum can is recycled, how long before that recycled can is back on the grocery shelf?"

Silence. Silence. Silence.

"Care to venture a guess?" Einstein asked. "Well, it takes only TWO MONTHS to completely recycle a can into a new, usable one. That is one fun fact!"

I guess Mr. Wright can't hear me after all, Einstein thought. *All this dead air is killing my show!*

"I'd like to thank my special guest, Mr. Wright. I hope everyone at home enjoyed this segment of **ANSWER... THAT... QUESTION**."

"Tough show today," Einstein told Marlon. "Mr. Wright was Mr. Totally Wrong."

Marlon shrugged, which is pretty tough to do when most of your body is tucked inside a shell. "Do all rodents talk to themselves, or is it just you?"

Einstein didn't let Marlon deter him. He KNEW his show was good. If only he could get the kids to tune in.

Einstein looked around the class-room. How could he do Tasty Tidbits without Ned cheering him on?

"Be right there!" Ned called from his locker. "I won't let you down."

Einstein smiled at his buddy. It was nice having a reliable friend.

EINSTEIN'S TASTY TIDBITS

Scientists disagree on whether the large clumps of sperm whales' undigested waste that sometimes wash up on shore are actually vomit or poop. The mass of waste is called ambergris and can float in the ocean for years. If found, ambergris is worth a fortune. And what is this whale waste prized for? It's used to make perfume.

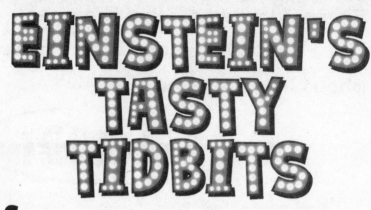

SOMETHING SMELLS GOOD.

CHAPTER SIX

NED ASKS EINSTEIN FOR HELP

Ms. Moreno burst into the classroom. "You wouldn't believe what I saw on TV last night! The hit show KIDS KNOW STUFF is looking all around the country for classes to compete, and they're holding auditions next week—here in town!"

Einstein usually tried to ignore Ms. Moreno, but was she talking about a GAME SHOW?

"The topics they cover on the show are the same subjects we've been studying all year. I can't imagine a better class to represent our town than this one!" Ms. Moreno did her little happy dance around her desk. "How about a class field trip to the audition? What do you say?"

"We say yes!" Bonnie shouted.

"Absolutely!" said Ricky.

Ned snuck over to the pencil sharpener to talk to Einstein.

"You've got to let me come!" Einstein said. "No one in this class knows more about game shows than I do."

"Ms. Moreno won't let you go on a field trip," Ned said. "There's no way."

"Please!" Einstein pleaded.

"I'm sorry, Einstein." Ned finished sharpening his pencil and went back to his desk.

"Okay, class!" Ms. Moreno said. "Take out your—"

But before she could finish the sentence, Ms. Moreno fell sound asleep at her desk.

Bonnie took a pillow from the reading loft and tucked it underneath Ms. Moreno's head. "Looks like Boerring Elementary doesn't get a shot at KIDS KNOW STUFF after all," Bonnie whispered.

"Instead of FUN facts, it's more like DONE facts," Ricky added.

Einstein perked up his tiny hamster

ears. *They need me,* he thought. *This is my moment to shine!*

"Don't get any ideas," Marlon said. "Nobody wants help from a hamster."

"Stop being so negative, Marlon. You'll never reach your full turtle potential that way."

Marlon tucked his head into his shell. "You're on your own, Einstein."

That whole hiding-in-the-shell thing is such a cop-out, Einstein thought.

Einstein climbed on his hamster wheel and started to run. Faster, then faster still. If he couldn't go to the game show with the class, at least he could help them study for the audition. He just had to figure out a way to get through to them.

EINSTEIN'S TASTY TIDBITS

Believe it or not, turtles have been around for 200 million years. They live on every continent except one. (Can you guess? It's

Antarctica.) All turtles lay their eggs on land; baby turtles have an egg tooth they use to break out of the egg when it's time to hatch. Like other reptiles, turtles are cold-blooded. They may have a reputation for being slow, but sea turtles swim faster than any other reptile. And on level ground, the smooth softshell turtle can sometimes outrun a human.

CHAPTER SEVEN

A FEW WORDS ABOUT MS. MORENO

The students had some theories about Ms. Moreno's constant napping:

- That Ms. Moreno suffered from a sleeping disorder.

- That her neighbors were incredibly loud and kept Ms. Moreno up all night.

- That Ms. Moreno was the rare

individual who needed eighteen hours of sleep each day.

Because Einstein had to stay at Ms. Moreno's sometimes, he knew the REAL reason for her daily catnaps. Ms. Moreno fell asleep throughout the day because she stayed up all night watching infomercials. Ms. Moreno loved hearing about the latest gadgets, weight-loss programs, and skin-cleansing regimens advertised late at night. Her wee hours were filled with juicers and yoga DVDs and ceramic knives. There just weren't enough hours in the day to learn about all these fabulous products.

It was too bad KIDS KNOW STUFF
wouldn't be asking any questions
about how to add sparkly beads to
your clothes because that was one
audition Ms. Moreno would ace.

EINSTEIN'S TASTY TIDBITS

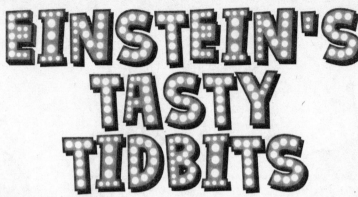

If you're wondering whether sleep disorders are real, they are. More than 20 percent of Americans suffer from chronic sleep loss. And not getting enough sleep can have disastrous effects: More than 1,500 people a year die because drivers fall asleep at the wheel.

Cars aren't the only place where it's deadly

to fall asleep. Tired people making critical decisions contributed to the *Exxon Valdez* oil spill, the Chernobyl nuclear disaster, and the *Challenger* space shuttle explosion. It's important to get your sleep!

CHAPTER EIGHT

EINSTEIN'S PLAN

"Your class will never pass the audition next week with Ms. Moreno asleep all the time," Einstein said. "So I'm stepping in as teacher."

"But no one else in the class can hear you," Ned said.

"That's why YOU have to translate," Einstein said.

"How's THAT going to work?"

Einstein patiently explained his plan.

"I'll review my notes with you, then YOU tell the other students what I'm saying."

"I can't tell them a hamster helped me study—they'll think I'm nuts! Besides, no one listens to me."

"But you're the smartest kid in class."

"You're just saying that because I'm the only one who talks to you."

"Come on," Einstein pleaded. "You and I are the best chance this class has to get on that show."

When Ned looked over at Ms. Moreno snoring at her desk, he had to agree Einstein had a point. "I'm not sure the other kids will believe the class hamster not only talks but has been taking notes," Ned said.

"Once they realize I can help them, they'll TOTALLY believe it."

Ned knew his classmates liked having Einstein in the class and liked taking him out of his cage to hold him. But Ned doubted any of them could comprehend a class hamster who knew more about the solar system than they did.

"Why don't I just teach the class?"
Ned suggested. "Don't you think that
makes more sense?"

"I WANT TO TEACH THE CLASS!"
Einstein cried. "IT'S MY DREAM!"

Ned had never seen a hamster have a tantrum before. It was NOT a pretty sight.

"Okay, okay," Ned said. "I'll translate for you."

"Good! Let me just freshen up backstage."

Ned slowly approached Ms. Moreno's desk. This was a terrible idea.

"Um...I have a plan for how we can ace the audition without Ms. Moreno," Ned told the class. "But it's pretty hard to believe."

Bonnie looked up from her comic book. Ricky put away his phone.

"I found someone who can tutor us," Ned said. "Someone who's been in our classroom all along."

Bonnie looked around. Who was Ned talking about?

CUPCAKES ARE NOT VEGETABLES

"This is it," Einstein told Marlon. "The day EVERYONE gets to play **ANSWER...THAT...QUESTION.**" Marlon let out a sigh. "You don't have a game show," the turtle said for the millionth time. "You answer your own questions."

But Einstein wasn't listening. His moment of fame was finally here.

"You probably won't be able to hear him, so I'll translate," Ned said to the class. "His name is—"

Ms. Moreno suddenly snorted herself awake.

"Is everybody ready to talk about Mars?" she asked. "There are so many amazing facts about the planets!"

"NO, no, no!" Einstein cried. "It's MY turn to teach, not yours! Go back to sleep! Let me get you a glass of warm milk!"

"Ned," Ms. Moreno said, "since you're up here, why don't you share a few facts about Mars? They might come in handy on KIDS KNOW STUFF."

Ned glanced over at Einstein. He had never seen a hamster look so sad.

EINSTEIN'S TASTY TIDBITS

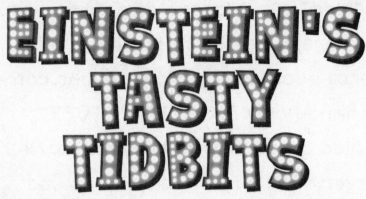

The planet Mars is home to something that may sound like an alien but isn't—the mysterious dust devil. Similar to tornadoes, dust devils are columns of wind that move along the surface of a planet when the ground gets warm. Earth has dust devils too, but the ones on Mars can be up to 50 times as wide and 10 times as high as dust devils here on Earth.

CHAPTER NINE

WHAT A BUMMER!

"**S**top lying there like a lump. You're scaring me," Marlon told Einstein.

But Einstein didn't answer. Instead he buried himself in the little cave of shredded paper in his cage. He gathered together a pile of ~~poop~~ food to play with as he stared out into the classroom.

Look at them, Einstein thought as

he watched the students. *They're so lucky—learning new facts about the world. And I was ALMOST the one to teach them.*

"Here comes someone to break up the pity party," Marlon said.

Einstein sat up with a start as

Principal Decker walked into the room
carrying Twinkles. He moved several
of Ms. Moreno's plants and cleared a
space on the shelf for Twinkles's tank.
When Twinkles slithered to the side
closest to Einstein, the hamster
buried himself deeper into his home-
made cave.

"Hello-o-o-o-o," Twinkles hissed.
"You look like you need a hug."

Einstein ignored the despicable python.

"Just a little squeeze," Twinkles continued. "You'll feel so much better."

To Einstein's surprise, Marlon piped up from his plastic lagoon. "Leave him alone," Marlon said. "Einstein's having a bad day."

Twinkles ignored the turtle.

"Just a teeny tiny hug," Twinkles said. "I guarantee it'll help."

From inside his cave, Einstein peeked out at Twinkles. He had to admit a hug DID sound good.

WAIT! What was he thinking? Twinkles was trouble. Twinkles was evil.

"Come on," Marlon told Einstein.
"It's only a matter of time before Ms.
Moreno falls asleep again. Maybe you
ARE the one to help them."

Marlon was right. Enough moping.
Einstein had to help the class prepare.

"Are you sure?" Twinkles asked one
more time. "Just a little cuddle?"

Einstein went back to his notes. Not even Twinkles could distract him today.

Principal Decker clapped his hands to get the class's attention. "Ms. Moreno told me about the game show audition next week. I think trying out for KIDS KNOW STUFF is a great idea. This could bring Boerring Elementary national attention!" He pointed to Twinkles's terrarium on the shelf. "Twinkles and I are behind you 100 percent."

"This has nothing to do with Twinkles," Einstein shouted. "I'M the game show expert around here!"

"Not according to him," Marlon said.

Twinkles gave Einstein a little wink, which is difficult to do when you don't have eyelids.

Einstein buried himself deeper into his shredded-paper hiding place. It felt terrible not to be wanted.

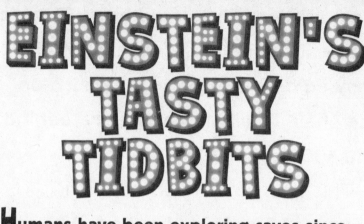

EINSTEIN'S TASTY TIDBITS

Humans have been exploring caves since the beginning of time. Mammoth Cave in Kentucky is the world's longest cave system with 390 miles of passages.

Stalactites form when water drips in limestone caves. Some of the mineral-rich water falls on the floor of the cave,

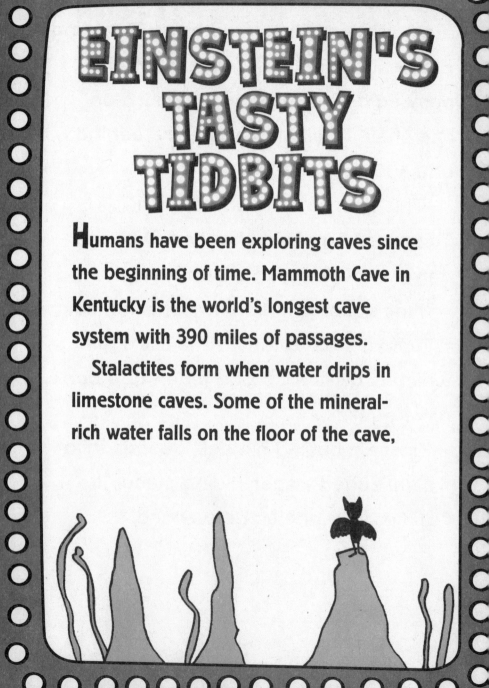

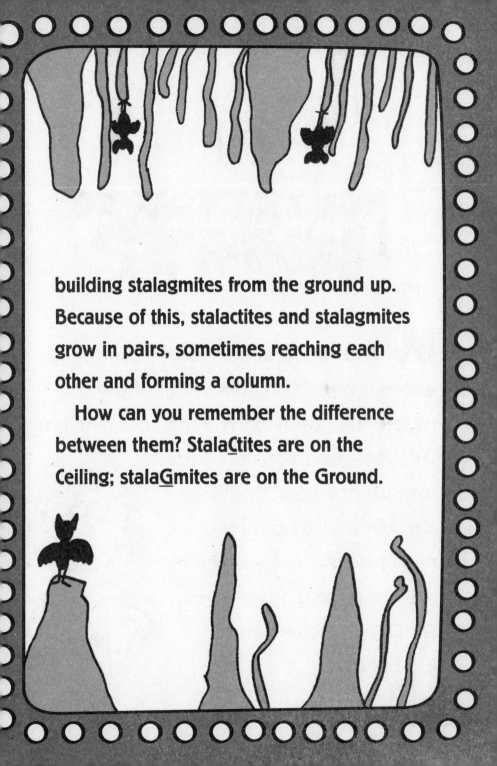

building stalagmites from the ground up. Because of this, stalactites and stalagmites grow in pairs, sometimes reaching each other and forming a column.

How can you remember the difference between them? Stala<u>C</u>tites are on the Ceiling; stala<u>G</u>mites are on the Ground.

CHAPTER TEN

YOU WANT US TO WHAT?

Ms. Moreno gathered her students around her. "You just heard how much this audition means to Principal Decker—and to me. If anyone wants to study over the weekend, it might really help our chances."

Bonnie rolled her eyes; Ricky muttered under his breath.

On a
Saturday?
I don't
think so...

Ned raised his hand. "Can I take
Einstein home for the weekend?"

Einstein peeked out from his hiding
place. *NOW you're talking.*

Ms. Moreno looked at the sign-up
sheet and told Ned it was Bonnie's turn.

When the bell rang, Ned approached
Bonnie and asked if he could take
Einstein home instead.

"What's so important about this
weekend? Is Einstein going to help
you study for KIDS KNOW STUFF?"
Bonnie teased.

Ned couldn't admit that was
EXACTLY why he wanted to take
Einstein home.

"Okay," Bonnie relented. "I'll take
him home another time."

Ned thanked Bonnie and gathered up his things.

For Einstein, helping Ned cram all weekend was a dream come true.

"Have fun," Marlon called. "See you Monday."

Einstein didn't bother saying good-
bye to Twinkles.

This weekend was going to be so
much better than last weekend, when
none of the students volunteered to
take him and he had to go home with
Ms. Moreno. While Einstein's classmates
were playing soccer and video games,
he was stuck watching infomercials
about pasta makers and weed whackers.
By the time he got back to school
that Monday, Einstein had sworn off
infomercials forever.

But this was a weekend playing
ANSWER ... THAT ... QUESTION
with Ned! Einstein vowed that Ned
would be the star student at next
week's audition.

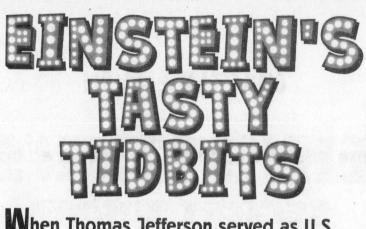

EINSTEIN'S TASTY TIDBITS

When Thomas Jefferson served as U.S. ambassador to France, he was introduced to macaroni on a trip to Italy. He loved it so much that he ordered a pasta machine to be shipped back to the United States. As the country's third president, he was the first to serve macaroni at the White House. In his papers at the Library of Congress, there's a pasta recipe written in Thomas Jefferson's own hand.

DECLARATION OF INDEPENDENCE

MACARONI AND CHEESE

CHAPTER ELEVEN

EINSTEIN'S
SECRET TUNNEL

Einstein packed for his weekend with Ned, making sure not to forget his study guide.

Ned knew hamsters were great at tunneling, but what he DIDN'T know was that Einstein had a complex system of passages running underneath the school. Mr. Wright had almost caught Einstein several times, but so far the security of Einstein's secret library hadn't been breached.

Einstein headed to the small opening under the water fountain, then made his way over to his library in the janitor's closet. He pulled out several volumes from his ancestors' study, hidden for generations in the insulation behind the wall. If he was going to teach the class with Ned on Monday morning, he'd need all the information he could carry.

Einstein sharpened his pencil, packed up his pencil case, then stuffed all the data into his cheek pouches before heading back to the classroom. His notes were a bit soggy, but they'd dry off soon enough. Lastly, he logged on to the class computer to check a few final facts on Hamsterpedia. (An informative site that's password protected: hamsters only.)

By the time Ned was ready to leave, Einstein was exhausted, but not too tired to notice a slip of paper sticking out of Ned's book. "What's that?"

"It's nothing," Ned answered.

Einstein could feel the envy growing inside him. "It's your permission slip for the audition next week, isn't it?"

Ned blushed with embarrassment.

"The whole class is taking a field trip to a game show." Einstein pouted. "Everyone except me!"

Ned pressed his face against Einstein's tank. "We can study for the audition all weekend, okay? It'll be fun."

Ned didn't need to remind Einstein that sulking wouldn't help the class next week. It was time for Einstein to stop feeling sorry for himself and get to work.

EINSTEIN'S TASTY TIDBITS

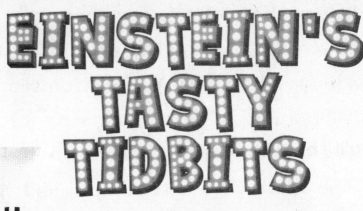

Hamsters are usually solitary animals. In the wild, they are nocturnal (active at night) as opposed to diurnal (active during the day). They can often run as fast backward as they can forward. Hamsters' teeth grow constantly, which means they have to grind them down so they don't get too long. A hamster is able to carry half its body weight in its cheek pouches. When their cheek pouches are full, their head can be two or three times its normal size.

CHAPTER TWELVE

SLEEPOVER AT NED'S

"**O**kay," Ned said after dinner. (Meat loaf for Ned, sunflower seeds for Einstein.) "Let's get started on your notes."

Einstein had never heard such eloquent words. He outlined all the subjects he had covered in his show and pored through the notes his parents and grandparents had left him. He quizzed Ned for hours, barely letting him take a dessert break.

When Ned went to bed, Einstein stayed up to outline more fun facts

for tomorrow's game of **ANSWER . . .
THAT . . . QUESTION**.

The next morning, Ned wanted to
play video games, but Einstein put his
hamster foot down. "What about the
audition?" Einstein asked. "There's so
much material to cover."

"I need a break," Ned complained.
"I can't study ALL the time."

"Of course you can!" Einstein
shouted. "I do!"

"I'll just play for a little while,"
Ned said.

"But yesterday you won a year's
supply of chocolate chip cookies!"
Einstein said. "You're my best
contestant!"

"I'm your ONLY contestant," Ned said.

"How about a Lightning Round? It'll be quick," Einstein pleaded.

"That's why it's called a Lighting Round." Ned laughed. "I'll be back soon."

Einstein immediately jumped on his wheel for some exercise. Didn't Ned know how important this audition was?

Half an hour later, Ned returned. "Okay," he said. "I'm ready."

Yay! Einstein thought. *My study partner is back!*

Ned and Einstein spent the rest of the day playing **ANSWER** ... **THAT** ... **QUESTION**.

"I have to admit," Ned said, "this game is pretty helpful."

All the years of Einstein collecting facts about science and nature and geography and history were paying off.

"You need a reward for all your hard work," Ned said.

Don't say it, Einstein thought. *You don't mean—*

Ned held up a strawberry.

"From the garden?" Einstein asked.

"From the garden," Ned answered.

"With the green still on?" Einstein asked.

"With the green still on," Ned answered.

Ned was the greatest kid on the planet.

EINSTEIN'S TASTY TIDBITS

Exercise not only helps your body but also your mind. When you exercise, your brain releases endorphins, brain chemicals called neurotransmitters. Endorphins relieve stress, help you feel better, and decrease feelings of pain in your body. Another way to increase endorphins in your body? Laughter—and lots of it.

CHAPTER THIRTEEN

TRAGEDY STRIKES

After playing **ANSWER...THAT... QUESTION** all weekend, Ned made his way through the ivy on the school entrance and put Einstein's tank on the shelf.

"So you're sure I can teach today?" Einstein asked. "You're not too embarrassed to translate?"

"I AM embarrassed, but I know

how important it is to you." Ned almost slipped on the puddle Ms. Moreno left when she watered her plants.

Wait until Marlon hears about my weekend, Einstein thought. *He's not going to believe it!*

Einstein looked around the turtle tank but couldn't spot his friend. Was he hiding behind the plastic palm tree? Einstein waited until no one was looking, then climbed out of his tank.

And how are YOU doing this morning?

"Marlon!" he cried. "I've got so much to tell you." He still couldn't find Marlon anywhere.

"Looking for someone?" Twinkles asked.

"What have you done with Marlon?" Einstein shouted. "Cough him up now!"

"That's not going to happen," Twinkles said. "But perhaps you'd like to say hello to your little friend." When Twinkles opened his mouth, Einstein thought he saw the top of Marlon's head.

HELP!

While Einstein was having the greatest weekend of his life playing **ANSWER ... THAT ... QUESTION** with Ned, poor Marlon was playing the part of Twinkles's midnight snack.

"What's the matter?" Ned asked as he ran over. "I could hear you screaming from outside."

Einstein pointed to the python.

"Twinkles ate Marlon?" Ned shook his head. "Boy, that shell is going to hurt on the way out."

"He was my friend," Einstein said sadly.

"Friends are important," Ned said. "You want me to help?"

"No," Einstein answered. "I've got

this." He crept across the shelf toward Twinkles's tank.

"I don't feel so good," Twinkles said as he coiled himself in the corner.

Einstein climbed into Twinkles's tank. Was the python really sick or was this another trap?

"Be careful!" Ned cried.

Einstein approached the groaning python and cautiously pried open Twinkles's mouth.

"Marlon!" Einstein called. "Are you in here? Come out! I can't hold open his mouth much longer!"

Marlon hurried as fast as a turtle inside a python can hurry.

Suddenly Twinkles sat up with a

smile. "Einstein," he hissed. "I see you've joined us for dessert."

Einstein felt the python grab him and slowly start to squeeze.

"There we are," Twinkles whispered. "Just relax."

The python's grip tightened around Einstein.

CAN ANYBODY HEAR ME?

"I DO feel a bit sleepy," Einstein said.

Suddenly the python's grip loosened. Ned had grabbed Twinkles and was unwinding him with both hands.

"Come on!" Ned said.

Einstein struggled to free himself from Twinkles's deadly grip.

"Let's get you out of here," Ned said.

"Not without Marlon." Einstein gathered his strength and pried open Twinkles's jaw one more time. "Marlon! Hurry up!"

There was nothing worse than sitting around waiting for one reptile to cough up another one.

"He's stuck!" Einstein shouted.

Ned grabbed Twinkles from behind.

He'd learned the Heimlich maneuver
at the Y's first-aid class last summer
and still remembered how to do it.

Marlon flew out of Twinkles's mouth
like a soggy bullet and landed in Ms.
Moreno's fern. As soon as he made

sure Marlon was okay, Ned hurried to put Twinkles back in his tank. He couldn't imagine what kind of detention Principal Decker would give him if he caught him harming his beloved python.

"Ouch," Twinkles moaned. "That really hurt."

"That's what you get for eating a schoolmate," Einstein answered.

"Remember when I said 'nobody wants help from a hamster'?" Marlon asked. "I was totally, 100 percent wrong. Thank you, Einstein."

"Don't thank me. Thank Ned. He saved my life too." Ned was a hero! Now the other kids would DEFINITELY see what a great kid he was.

But the other kids were back from recess, listening to Tommy tell yet another story about his new bike. None of them had noticed Ned's bravery. Einstein could see the disappointment on Ned's face.

Einstein turned his attention to
Marlon, who was still a bit stunned.
"I never should've left you alone
with Twinkles."

Marlon tried to smile. "Did you and
Ned study this weekend? Is he ready
to help you teach today?"

Einstein had been so focused on FACTS, FACTS, FACTS that he'd forgotten about Ned's feelings, just like he'd forgotten about Marlon's. He'd overlooked one essential FACT: It was important to be a good friend.

Einstein glanced at Ms. Moreno's desk. Her speech was getting slower, her head heavy.

"Are you ready to finally teach the class?" Marlon asked.

But Einstein had a new and better idea to put into action.

EINSTEIN'S TASTY TIDBITS

There are about half a million different types of flowering plants in the world. Around 600 species are carnivorous, or flesh eating. Some plants don't start off carnivorous but become that way when the soil has little to no nutrients. The plants capture and eat small prey like insects. But some carnivorous plants capture and devour frogs, birds, and even rodents.

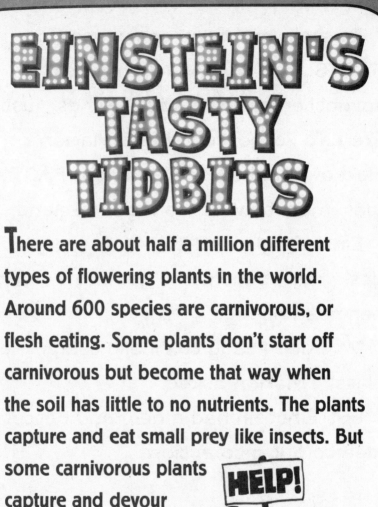

HELP!

CHAPTER FOURTEEN

A
SWITCHEROO

"**I** know we had it all planned," Einstein said, "but I've changed my mind. I want YOU to get the class ready for tomorrow's audition instead."

"ME?" Ned exclaimed. "No way!"

"You know the material as well as I do."

"But why?" Ned said. "You've been waiting to teach the class your whole life."

For the first time in their friendship, Einstein lied to Ned. "I'm still pretty woozy from Twinkles almost squeezing me to death. YOU have to help the class ace the audition." He pointed to Ms. Moreno, now sound asleep at her desk. "Go!"

Ned hesitated.

"Go!" Marlon added.

Ned shyly approached Bonnie.

"Um," Ned began softly. "I want to help us study for KIDS KNOW STUFF."

Bonnie looked at Ned suspiciously. "You're smart, but not THAT smart."

"Why should we listen to you?" Tracy added.

"Because we have a real chance at this," Ned said.

Ned looked over at Einstein, who gave him a hamster-size thumbs-up. *You can do this,* Einstein thought.

Bonnie had never paid much attention to Ned before, but he seemed to really care about the class. And besides, she hadn't studied over the weekend and could use all the help she could get. She turned to her friends. "What do we have to lose?"

Einstein shouted from his cage like a cheerleader.

Ned took out his notes and talked to the class about mosquitoes and whales and state capitals. He talked to them about the solar system and presidents, even throwing in a few facts about hamsters.

When he looked at his classmates, Ned was happy to see they were not only taking notes but smiling. He mouthed the words THANK YOU to Einstein.

"But, Einstein," said a still groggy Marlon. "No one will ever know about *your* game show."

Einstein watched Ned explaining a Tasty Tidbit to Ricky. "There'll be other times," Einstein said.

"My thoughts exactly," Twinkles hissed from his tank.

EINSTEIN'S TASTY TIDBITS

Jupiter is the biggest planet in the solar system, so big that all the other planets could fit inside it. The Great Red Spot on Jupiter is actually a humongous storm—more than three times the size of Earth.

Jupiter may be large, but it spins quickly on its axis. A day on Jupiter isn't 24 hours like on Earth, but only about 9 hours and 55 minutes. That planet's moving fast!

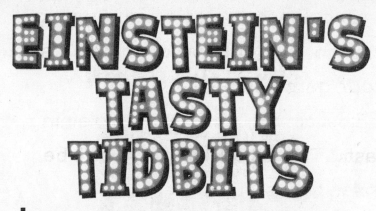

CHAPTER FIFTEEN

FIELD TRIP

As soon as Principal Decker finished the morning announcements, Ms. Moreno grabbed her purse. "Is everyone ready to hit the road?"

The class hadn't had a field trip in months, and they were all looking forward to it.

"Ms. Moreno's not driving, is she?" Bonnie asked.

Ricky told her that one of the

regular bus drivers would be taking
them to the studio today. Bonnie
breathed a sigh of relief.

When Ned went to say good-bye to
Einstein, he found him wearing his full
game show getup.

"You know you can't come, right?"
Ned asked.

"I figured it was worth a try."
Einstein pulled off his wig. "Will you at
least take pictures of the set?"

"Of course."

"The stage? The lights? The buzzers?"

"It's just an audition," Ned said. "Wish us luck."

"You don't need luck. You studied." But Einstein crossed his fingers anyway.

Waiting for the class to get back to school was the worst four hours of Einstein's life. He watched TV, did some research on the class computer, played Yahtzee with Marlon. (He let Marlon win.) He went down to the Science Center to make sure Twinkles's tank was secure. Without Principal Decker parading the python

120

around, Twinkles seemed much less menacing—until he saw Einstein hiding behind the ant farm. Twinkles shot the hamster a GET OFF MY TURF look that had Einstein scurrying through the tunnel system to the safety of his tank.

When Einstein finally heard the bus pull into the parking lot, he thought he might explode with excitement. Did the class make the cut?

"WELL?"

Ned couldn't hide the satisfaction on his face. "We made the finals! Our class will compete in a new trivia segment of KIDS KNOW STUFF. And it's all because of **YOU!**"

Einstein thought about his long line of hamster relatives and how proud they'd be. There was nothing trivial about fun facts—any class hamster could tell you that.

"So many of the questions they asked were ones you made me study," Ned said. "We were totally prepared and it showed."

Bonnie approached Ned as he fed Einstein a celebratory handful of kibble.

"You knew so many of the answers," Bonnie said. "Did you study with someone this weekend?"

"Me, me, me!" Einstein shouted, knowing Bonnie couldn't hear him.

"I just like learning new facts, that's all," Ned told her shyly.

"Well, you're the reason we made the cut," Bonnie said. "Nice going."

"Did you hear that?" Ned asked when Bonnie left.

"Looks like you found a new study partner," Einstein added.

"I'm so proud of you," Ms. Moreno told the class. "I really think those practice drills we did together made all the difference."

"You slept through every one!" Einstein shouted. "Ned did all the work, not you!" Einstein was on his way to give Ms. Moreno a piece of his mind when Marlon held him back.

"Let it go," Marlon said.

Einstein shook his head sadly. "She didn't do a THING."

"I know," Marlon said. "I know."

Einstein looked over at Ned, surrounded by his new friends.

"Lights! Camera! Action! I can't wait to see how the class does on the real game show," Ms. Moreno said. "Why, I bet—"

CLUNK.

Bonnie turned off the light so Ms. Moreno could nap. When Principal Decker hurried into the room to congratulate the class, he was shocked to see Ms. Moreno asleep at her desk.

WE ARE THE CHAMPIONS,
MY FRIENDS!

"Is Ms. Moreno okay?" he asked.
"Why is she sleeping?"

Ned explained that Ms. Moreno was
exhausted from working around the
clock to help them pass the audition.
Principal Decker covered Ms. Moreno
with a quilt from the reading loft,

then called in one of the lunch ladies, who brought in a giant chocolate cake. (Of course the first piece went to Twinkles.)

"Last year's class certainly knew what they were doing when they named you Einstein," Ned said. "You're a genius."

"Right back at you," Einstein answered.

EINSTEIN'S TASTY TIDBITS

Scientists believe that ants first appeared on Earth about 130 million years ago. The mass of all the ants on Earth is equal to the mass of all the humans. There are more than 1.5 million ants on the planet for every person! Believe it or not, there are over 12,000 different ant species, and they're on all the continents except one. (Yes, you guessed it—Antarctica again.) In the Amazon rainforest, one acre alone is home to more than 3.5 million ants.

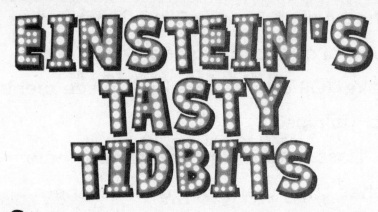

CHAPTER SIXTEEN

NED'S SURPRISE

Einstein couldn't believe his good luck. Not only did his class ace the audition, but Ned volunteered to take Einstein home for the weekend again. He watched TV next to his friend and even got to know some of Ned's other pets. It was especially nice to spend time with Benjamin the ferret, who was quite good at impersonations.

(But Einstein did notice a few of his belongings were missing afterward.)

"You let me lead our class to victory," Ned told Einstein. "So now it's my turn to do something nice for you."

Ned made Einstein close his eyes as he carried him into the kitchen.

When Ned set Einstein down, Einstein couldn't believe what he saw. The kitchen table had been converted into an elaborate game show set, complete with lights, podiums, and even a stage.

Einstein pointed to Ned's action figures. "Are those CONTESTANTS?"

"Yes," Ned said. "But I want to play, too."

Einstein was in awe of how much work Ned had put in.

"I have no idea how, but we're going to find a way to sneak you into the REAL studio next month," Ned

continued. "You deserve to be there when our class competes for the grand prize."

OUR class—it was the nicest thing Einstein had ever heard. When Ned hit PLAY on his mom's laptop, lively music filled the room. Einstein was so overwhelmed he could barely talk. "Is that a THEME SONG?"

Ned grinned. "Are you ready to finally host your show?"

Einstein took a deep breath and stepped to the center of the stage. Ned was the best friend he'd ever had, and that was one fun fact he wouldn't trade for all the others in the world.

"Ladies and gentlemen!" Einstein said. "Welcome to this special edition of **ANSWER ... THAT ... QUESTION**!"

This time when Ned hit PLAY, the kitchen filled with thunderous applause.

"Is everyone ready for a Lightning Round?" Einstein continued. "For those of you new to our show, a Lightning Round means a contestant has to answer rapid-fire questions before his or her time is up. Think you're ready?"

"Absolutely!" Ned yelled.

Einstein knew a lot of things, but what he knew most of all was that he and Ned would lead their class to victory next month. He knew they'd find a way to win the top prize— together.

"Well, if you're ready," Einstein said, "let the games begin!"

ANSWER... THAT... QUESTION!

⚡ LIGHTNING ROUND ⚡

1. What United States president was an ambassador to France and brought back macaroni from Europe?

2. What is undigested whale vomit used for?

3. Are reptiles cold-blooded or warm-blooded?

4. What part of the world has the highest concentration of mosquitoes?

5. How do pythons kill their prey?

6. Why do hamsters grind their teeth?

7. How long ago did the first turtles live?

8. What planet has giant dust devils?

9. Do stalagmites grow up or down in caves?

10. The *Exxon Valdez* oil spill, the Chernobyl nuclear disaster, and the *Challenger* space shuttle explosion were all linked to what?

11. What is the largest planet in the solar system?

12. Who was the third president of the United States?

13. What is the capital of Texas?

14. Every continent has turtles and ants except for one. Name it.

15. What is a carnivorous plant?

16. When you exercise, your body creates what kind of brain chemicals?

17. Which mosquitoes bite, male or female?

18. How many hours a day do ferrets sleep?

19. Where is the largest cave system in the world?

20. Hamsters can carry half their body weight in their what?

21. What are animals called that are active in the day?

22. If it's not recycled, a can clutters up the planet for how many years?

23. The mass of all the ants on Earth is equal to the mass of what?

Ned got them all right. See if you did too.

1. THOMAS JEFFERSON

2. MAKING PERFUME

3. COLD-BLOODED

4. THE ARCTIC

5. BY SQUEEZING THEM

6. TO KEEP THEM FROM GROWING TOO LONG

7. 200 MILLION YEARS AGO

8. MARS

9. THEY GROW UP FROM THE GROUND

10. SLEEP DEPRIVATION

11. JUPITER

12. THOMAS JEFFERSON

13. AUSTIN

14. ANTARCTICA

15. ONE THAT IS FLESH EATING

16. ENDORPHINS

17. FEMALE

18. TWENTY

19. KENTUCKY

20. CHEEK POUCHES

21. DIURNAL

22. 100

23. ALL THE HUMANS ON EARTH

SPECIAL FEATURES

BLOOPERS AND DELETED SCENES

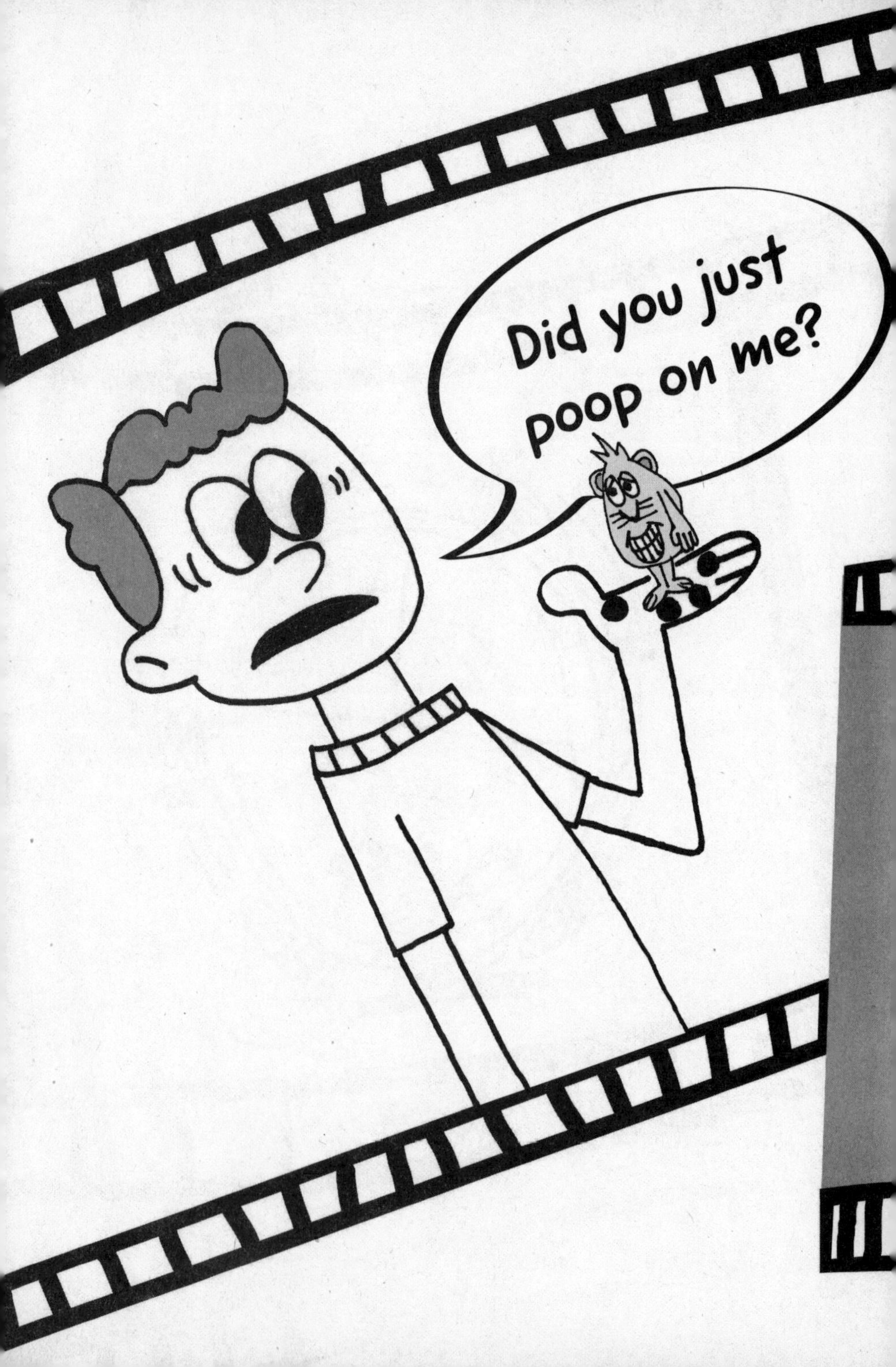
Did you just poop on me?

146

FIND OUT MORE

Want to find out more information about my Tasty Tidbits? Explore your local library or check out these online sites:

MOSQUITOES: www.nature.com/news/2010/100721/full/466432a.html (*Nature*)

FERRETS: www.dfg.ca.gov/wildlife/nongame/nuis_exo/ferret/ferret.html (*California Department of Fish and Game*)

PYTHONS: www.sandiegozoo.org/animalbytes/t-python.html (*San Diego Zoo*)

RECYCLING: maine.gov/spo/recycle/mainerecycles/enduringlitter.htm (*Maine State Planning Office*)
http://earth911.com/news/2007/04/02/benefits-of-aluminum-can-recycling/ (*Earth 911*)

WHALES: www.bbc.co.uk/news/uk-england-dorset-19431540 (*BBC News*)
news.nationalgeographic.com/news/2012/08/120830-ambergris-charlie-naysmith-whale-vomit-science/ (*National Geographic*)

SLEEP DISORDERS: healthysleep.med.harvard.edu/healthy/matters/consequences/sleep-performance-and-public-safety (*Healthy Sleep*)
www.webmd.com/sleep-disorders/features/toll-of-sleep-loss-in-america (*WebMD*)

DUST DEVILS: science.nasa.gov/science-news/science-at-nasa/2005/14jul_dustdevils/ (*NASA Science News*)
www.weatherquestions.com/What_are_dust_devils.htm (WeatherQuestions.com)

CAVES: www.nps.gov/maca/index.htm (National Park Service)
science.howstuffworks.com/environmental/earth/geology/stalactite-stalagmite.htm (How Stuff Works)

MACARONI: recipes.howstuffworks.com/menus/who-invented-macaroni-and-cheese.htm (*How Stuff Works*)

HAMSTERS: a-z-animals.com/animals/hamster/ (*A-Z Animals*)

EXERCISE: science.howstuffworks.com/life/inside-the-mind/emotions/exercise-happiness2.htm (*How Stuff Works*)

CARNIVOROUS PLANTS: ngm.nationalgeographic.com/2010/03/carnivorous-plants/zimmer-text (*National Geographic*)
phys.org/news204438872.html (*PhysOrg.com*)

JUPITER: www.nasa.gov/audience/forstudents/k-4/stories/what-is-jupiter-k4.html (*NASA*)

ANTS: http://insects.about.com/od/antsbeeswasps/a/10-cool-facts-about-ants.htm (*About.com*)

GOFISH

JANET TASHJIAN

What's your favorite thing about Einstein the Class Hamster?
I think the thing I love most about Einstein is that he's living in his own little world. You could say he's a bit delusional hosting a game show or thinking he should be running the classroom, but I love his determination and spunk. Jake's illustrations make me so happy; my favorites are Einstein with his hand in his pocket and his deadpan look to the camera. Einstein is one of my favorite characters, hands down.

What is your favorite "fun fact" in this book and why?
I love all the Tasty Tidbits; doing research for them is one of the best parts of writing this series. My favorite is probably the one about Thomas Jefferson serving macaroni and cheese at the White House. When we show that slide on school visits, kids always laugh at the illustration of Thomas Jefferson holding the Declaration of Independence in one hand and a recipe for mac and cheese in the other.

Do you watch any trivia game shows on TV? And if so, which one?

I don't watch a lot of trivia game shows, although Jake and I are an amazing team when we play *Hollywood Game Night*. We talk about going on it all the time. We're such movie nerds, we'd be unstoppable on that show.

What did you want to be when you grew up?

Students ask me this all the time, and I wish I had a better answer. When I was young, I was too busy playing, reading, and studying to think about career goals. I envy people who knew what they wanted to be by age ten. I was not one of them.

When did you realize you wanted to be a writer?

Several years ago I traveled around the world, and when I got back to the States, I had to fill in some forms. One asked for my occupation and I put down "writer," even though I'd never done anything more than dabble. But deep down, I always felt being a writer would be the greatest job in the world. It took me several years to make that dream a reality.

What's your first childhood memory?

I remember cooking candies in a little pan on a toy stove that I got for Christmas. I was maybe three. I'm not sure if I remember it or if I just saw the photograph so often that I think I do.

What's your most embarrassing childhood memory?

I was singing and dancing in a school assembly with my first-grade class when my shoe fell off. I kept going without the shoe, hopping around the stage—the show must go on.

What was your worst subject in school?
I always did well in school, but for some reason I forgot all my math skills and now can barely multiply. I'd love to know where all my math skills went.

What was your first job?
I've had dozens of jobs since I was sixteen—working on assembly lines, babysitting, washing dishes, waiting tables, delivering dental molds and telephone books, selling copy machines, working in a fabric store, painting houses. . . . I could fill a whole page with how many jobs I've had.

How did you celebrate publishing your first book?
By inviting my tenth-grade English teacher to my first book signing. The photo of the two of us from that day sits on my writing desk.

Where do you write your books?
Usually in my office on my treadmill desk. But because I often write in longhand, I end up writing everywhere—on the beach, in a coffee shop, wherever I am.

When you finish a book, who reads it first?
Always my editor, Christy Ottaviano. We've been doing books together for almost two decades; I consider her one of my closest friends.

How do you usually feel once you've completed a manuscript? Are you ever sad when a book you are writing is over?
Relieved! I don't really miss my characters; they're always with me.

Are you a morning person or a night owl?
I like waking up early and getting right to work. I'm too fried by the end of the day to get anything substantial done.

What's your idea of the best meal ever?
Something healthy and fresh, with lots of friends sitting around and talking. Definitely a chocolate dessert.

Which do you like better, cats or dogs?
I love dogs and have always had one. I'm allergic to cats, so I stay away from them. They don't seem as fun as dogs, anyway.

What do you value most in your friends?
Dependability and a sense of humor. All my friends are pretty funny.

Where do you go for peace and quiet?
I head to the woods. I'm there all the time. I love the beach, too.

What makes you laugh out loud?
My son. He's by far the funniest person I know.

What are you most afraid of?
I worry about all the normal mom things, like war, drunk drivers, and strange illnesses with no cures. I'm also afraid our culture is so invested in technology that we're veering away from basic things like nature. I worry about the implications down the road.

What time of the year do you like the best?
The summer, absolutely. I hate the cold.

If you were stranded on a desert island, who would you want for company?
My family.

If you could travel in time, where would you go?
To the future, to see how badly we've messed things up.

What's the best advice you have ever received about writing?
To do it as a daily practice, like running or meditation.

How do you react when you receive criticism?
My sales background and MFA workshops have left me with a very tough skin. If the feedback makes the book better, bring it on.

What do you want readers to remember about your books?
I want them to remember the characters as if they were old friends.

What would you do if you ever stopped writing?
Try to live my life without finding stories everywhere. For a job, I'd do some kind of design—anything from renovating houses to creating fabric.

What do you like best about yourself?
I'm not afraid to work.

What is your worst habit?
I hate to exercise.

What do you consider to be your greatest accomplishment?
How great my son is.

What do you wish you could do better?
Write a perfect first draft.

What would your readers be most surprised to learn about you?
I litter McDonald's trash out of my car window when I drive—KIDDING!

What is your favorite sound?
My son laughing really hard.

What is your idea of fun?
Seeing comedy or music in a tiny club.

Is there anything you'd like to confess?
I love dark chocolate.

What would your friends say if we asked them about you?
She acts like a fifteen-year-old boy.

What's on your list of things to do right now?
EXERCISE!

What do you think about when you're bored?
Story ideas.

How do you spend a rainy day?
Watching comedy.

Can you share a little-known fact about yourself?
I love to make collages.

GO FISH

JAKE TASHJIAN

Did you ever have a class hamster at school? Or a pet hamster at home?

I've never had a hamster at home, though we've always had dogs. I did have a class hamster in preschool named Sleepyhead. In my fifth-grade class there was Garfield the hedgehog, named after the comic-strip cat.

What is your favorite trivia game show on TV?

I don't really watch trivia shows, but I love the *Jeopardy!* parodies on *Saturday Night Live*. I've seen them all a million times.

What is your favorite illustration in the book and why?

My favorite is the one where Einstein is dressed like General MacArthur when he's helping Ned study. I love to draw Einstein in different costumes. I do it sometimes just for fun, not even for the books.

Einstein, the (mostly) talking hamster, is back, and it's time for the big leagues— hosting a very real TV game show!

KEEP READING FOR AN EXCERPT.

CHAPTER ONE

TIME TO COMPETE!

"**W**elcome, boys and girls, to a new episode of

ANSWER THAT QUESTION!

I'm your host, Einstein the class hamster, and we've got some great fun facts for you today. Ready, kids?"

Marlon looked around the empty classroom. Why did Einstein insist on starting each morning by talking to himself?

"Is that a yes, folks?" Einstein asked. "Who's ready to play?"

Marlon had hoped Ned would bail him out, but Ned was still at recess with the rest of the class. "**I'm ready!**" Marlon finally shouted.

"Our longtime champion has returned!" Einstein said into his mic. "Welcome back to the show, Marlon!"

Marlon reluctantly waved to the invisible audience.

"Marlon, here's your first question." Einstein glanced at his notes. "For fifty dollars and a chance at our

OXYMORONS:
SMALL CROWD

grand prize, is an alligator a reptile or an amphibian? You have ten seconds, and your time starts... **NOW!**"

Of course Marlon knew the answer. Alligators were reptiles, just like turtles. Einstein usually tried to make the first round a little tougher. Was this a trick question?

"**FIVE SECONDS!**"

Einstein called.

Maybe Einstein knew something Marlon didn't. Was there some new category alligators fell into? Did they get kicked out of the reptile group the same way poor Pluto got fired from the solar system? Maybe Marlon didn't know the answer to this question after all.

"Your time is up," Einstein said. "Care to venture a guess, Marlon?"

Marlon paced around, then took a deep breath. "Are they reptiles?"

OXYMORONS:
BAGGY TIGHTS

"Marlon, why are you answering that question with a question? **Of COURSE** alligators are reptiles, just like you." Einstein turned to face the camera, which was also nonexistent. "We'll be right back after this word from our sponsor. And stay tuned for a new Tasty Tidbit!"

Einstein scurried closer to Marlon. "Are you okay, buddy? You seem a little off your game today."

"I was confused," Marlon answered. "But everything's fine now."

"Everything's more than fine," Ned said as he approached the class pets. "Tomorrow our class competes on a national game show in front of a live audience! It's going to be great!"

Einstein tried to be happy for Ned and his other classmates, but it was hard to be enthusiastic when class pets weren't allowed on the field trip to cheer them on. He gave Ned a weak smile and changed the subject.

"Marlon just won fifty dollars in the first round of **ANSWER... THAT... QUESTION**," Einstein said. "You want to join him for round two?"

"I can't," Ned said. "I have to prepare for tomorrow."

"It's important to study," Einstein agreed.

"Oh, I'm not studying," Ned said.
"I'm figuring out a way to sneak you
into the television studio."

Einstein looked at Marlon.

Marlon looked at Einstein.

They both looked at Ned.

"The only reason our class made the finals is because you coached us," Ned said. "The class needs you there, and I'm determined to get you in."

Einstein couldn't believe the only student who could hear him was also the most dependable friend in the world. If anyone could get him into the studio tomorrow, it was Ned.

Ned bent down close to Einstein. "I'm going to try and sneak Marlon in too."

BOTH CLASS PETS? That would be amazing!

"Better rest up," Einstein told Marlon. "Looks like we might be going on a field trip."

"Is now a good time for me to

collect that fifty-dollar prize?" Marlon asked. "I **DID** win it fair and square."

But Einstein was too focused on the possibility of visiting a REAL game show.

He hoped Ned and his other classmates would figure out a way to get him in.